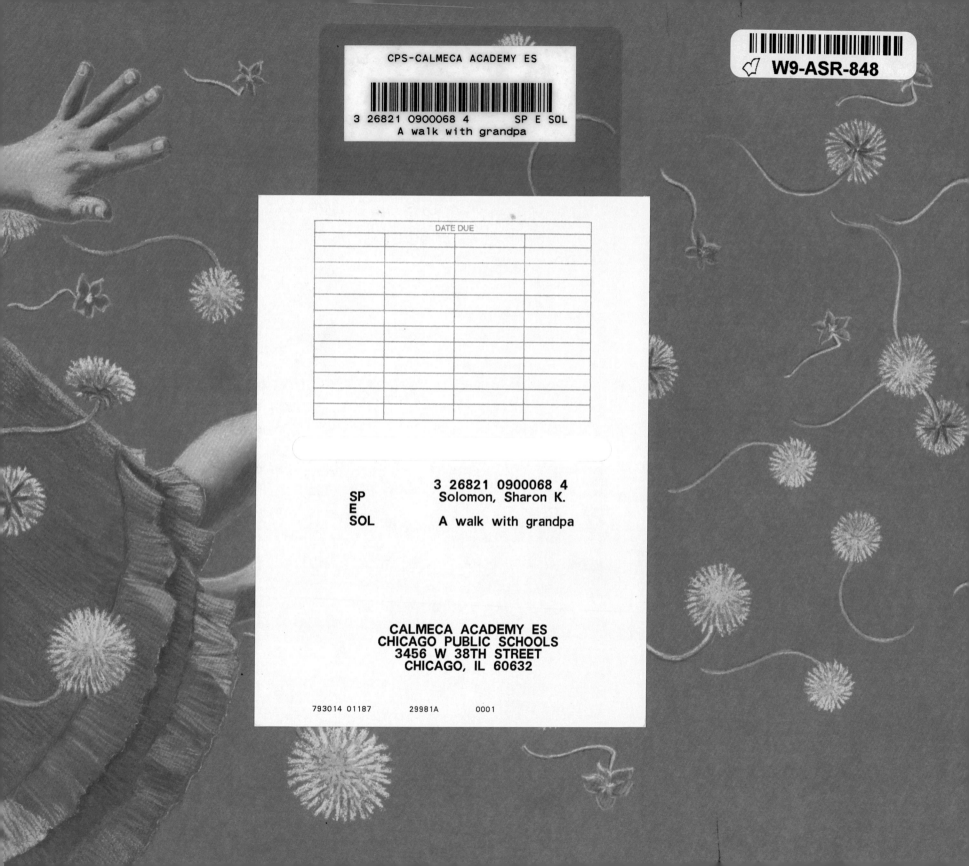

A Walk With Grandpa
Un paseo con abuelo

Written by/escrito por Sharon K. Solomon

Illustrated by /ilustrado por Pamela Barcita

A Walk With Grandpa
Un paseo con abuelo

To my wonderful husband Howard – Sharon
For José and Miranda – Pamela

To the woodlands, riverscapes and creatures of
Northwest River Park in Chesapeake, Virginia,
the inspiration for this visual journey.

Text ©2009 by Sharon K. Solomon
Illustration ©2009 by Pamela Barcita
Translation ©2009 by Raven Tree Press

Solomon, Sharon K.

A Walk With Grandpa / written by Sharon K. Solomon; illustrated by Pamela Barcita;
translated by Eida de la Vega = Un paseo con abuelo / escrito por Sharon K. Solomon;
ilustrado por Pamela Barcita; traducción al español de Eida de la Vega –
1st ed. – McHenry, IL, Raven Tree Press. 2009.

p. ; cm.

Full text translation in English and Spanish.
SUMMARY: Daniela and her grandpa take a walk in the woods and share what they mean to each other.

Bilingual Edition
ISBN: 978-1-932748-91-8   Hardcover
ISBN: 978-1-932748-90-1   Paperback

Audience: pre-K to 3rd grade.

1. Family/Multigenerational – Juvenile fiction. 2. Concepts/Opposites – Juvenile fiction.
3. Bilingual books – English and Spanish.
4. Spanish language materials – books. I. Illust. Barcita, Pamela. II. Title. III. Title: Un paseo con abuelo.

Library of Congress Control Number: 2008932221

Printed in Taiwan
10 9 8 7 6 5 4 3 2 1

First Edition

Free activities for this book are available at www.raventreepress.com

One sunny day, Daniela and her grandpa went for a walk.
They played a silly word game as they walked along.

Un día soleado, Daniela y su abuelo salieron de paseo.
Mientras caminaban, iban jugando un simpático juego de palabras.

"You are my sunshine,"
said Grandpa.

— *Eres mi rayo de sol*
— *dijo el abuelo.*

"You are my moonshine,"
giggled Daniela.

— *Eres mi rayo de luna*
— *dijo Daniela riéndose.*

5

"You are my earth."

— *Eres mi tierra.*

"You are my sky."
She squeezed his hand.

— Eres mi cielo — dijo
Daniela apretándole
la mano.

"You are my summer."

— *Eres mi verano.*

8

"You are my winter."

— *Eres mi invierno.*

"You are my question."

— *Eres mi pregunta.*

"And you are my answer."

— *Y tú eres mi respuesta.*

11

"You are my day."

— Eres mi día.

"You are my night."

— *Eres mi noche.*

"You are my hello."

— *Eres mi saludo.*

"You are my good-bye."

— *Eres mi despedida.*

15

"You are my lost."

— Eres lo que perdí.

"And you are my found."

— *Y tú eres lo que encontré.*

17

They sat on the big gray rock, looking down at the river.
Daniela kicked her feet as she watched their reflections in the water.

Se sentaron en una enorme roca gris, mirando hacia el río.
Daniela movió los pies mientras contemplaba su reflejo en el agua.

Then, she hugged her grandpa. "I love you, Pop Pop," she said. "And I love you, my little Tulip," said Grandpa.

Entonces abrazó a su abuelo. —Te quiero, abuelito — le dijo. —Y yo a ti, mi pequeño tulipán — dijo el abuelo.

Soon it was time to go home.
"You are my friend," said Daniela.

Pronto llegó la hora de regresar.
— Eres mi amigo — dijo Daniela.

"You are my pal,"
Grandpa replied.

— *Eres mi amiga*
— *replicó el abuelo.*

21

"You are my music."

— *Eres mi música.*

"You are my song."

— *Eres mi canción.*

"You are my hope."

— *Eres mi esperanza.*

"You are my wish."

— *Eres mi deseo.*

"You are my happy."

— *Eres mi felicidad.*

"You are my glad."

— *Eres mi alegría.*

27

"You are my super grandpa," Daniela said.

—*Eres mi súper abuelo* — *dijo Daniela.*

"And you are my wonderful granddaughter,"
Grandpa replied.

—Y tú eres mi nieta maravillosa
— replicó el abuelo.

29

"Let's walk again tomorrow," said Daniela.
Grandpa nodded with a smile.

—Vamos a dar otro paseo mañana
—dijo Daniela.
El abuelo asintió con una sonrisa.

Vocabulary / Vocabulario

Grandpa	*el abuelo*
Walk/to walk	*paseo/caminar*
Sunshine	*el rayo de sol*
Sky	*el cielo*
Summer	*el verano*
Winter	*el invierno*
Day	*el día*
Night	*la noche*
Music	*la música*
Song	*la canción*
Granddaughter	*la nieta*

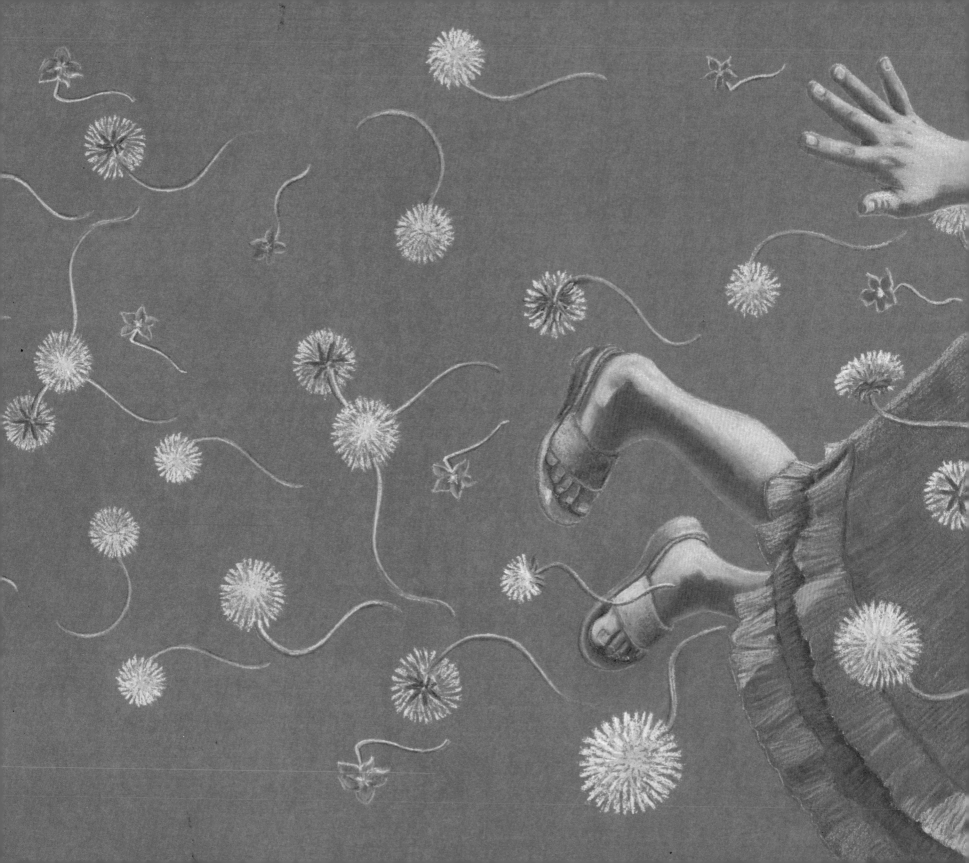